Please return or renew this item by the last date shown. There may be a charge if you fail to do so. Items can be returned to any Westminster library.

Telephone: Enquiries 020 7641 1?
Renewals (24 hour service) 02?
Online renewal service avai'
Web site: www.westminster.g

KT-420-272

QUE

WITHDRAWN

City of Westminster

Pearson Education Limited
Edinburgh Gate, Harlow,
Essex CM20 2JE, England
and Associated Companies throughout the world.

ISBN: 978-1-4058-5531-0

First published by Penguin Books 2000
This edition published 2008

12

Text copyright © Penguin Books Ltd 2000
This edition copyright © Pearson Education Ltd 2008
Opening illustration by Alan Fraser (Pennant Illustration)

Typeset by Graphicraft Ltd, Hong Kong
Set in 11/14pt Bembo
Printed in China
SWTC/12

Published by Pearson Education Ltd

Acknowledgements:
The publisher would like to thank the following for
their kind permission to reproduce their photographs:

Rex Shutterstock: Film Trust Production 3, 11, 15, 21, Moviestore Collection 31

Cover images: Front and back: **Ronald Grant Archive;**
CD Cover: Onbody: **Ronald Grant Archive**

Every effort has been made to trace the copyright holders and we apologise in advance
for any unintentional omissions. We would be pleased to insert the appropriate
acknowledgement in any subsequent edition of this publication.

For a complete list of the titles available in the Pearson English Readers series, please visit
www.pearsonenglishreaders.com. Alternatively, write to your local Pearson Education
office or to Pearson English Readers Marketing Department, Pearson Education,
Edinburgh Gate, Harlow, Essex CM20 2JE, England.

Contents

Introduction

'You can use a sword. You will fight well because you are a Gascon and my son. Fight when you are angry with somebody. But do not fight the King or the Cardinal!'

These are the words of young d'Artagnan's father, when his son leaves home for Paris. D'Artagnan wants to fight for his King and his country, but other fights come first. Who are the three musketeers, and why do they want to kill him? Why is the King angry with the Queen? Is the Cardinal the King's friend, or has he got other plans? And who is the beautiful 'Milady'?

Alexandre Dumas wrote *The Three Musketeers* in 1844, but everything in the story happened more than 200 years before that. Louis XIII was the King of France then, but he was very young. Cardinal Richelieu did nearly everything for him. When King Louis was fourteen, he married the daughter of the King of Spain. But for a time she was very friendly with the Duke of Buckingham, a friend of King Charles I of England.

The Duke of Buckingham tried to help the French Protestants. France was a Catholic country, but the Protestants took the city of La Rochelle from the King. The King and the Cardinal had to take the city back. The King's army used long guns – muskets. People with these guns were 'musketeers'.

Alexandre Dumas wrote a lot of books, and his most exciting stories are the most famous. *The Three Musketeers* and *The Count of Monte Cristo* are also films.

Chapter 1   At an Inn in Meung

'Well, all right,' said d'Artagnan's father. 'Go to Paris. You are only eighteen years old, but you are not a child. I cannot give you much money, but you can have my horse. And I will write a letter to my old friend, de Tréville. He is a Gascon★ too, and he and I were friends in the army. Now he is the captain of the King's musketeers.

'You can use a sword. You will fight well because you are a Gascon and my son. Fight when you are angry with somebody. But do not fight the King or the Cardinal!'

With these words, the older man gave his sword to his son. Then he turned away. He didn't want his son to see him cry.

D'Artagnan's mother cried too, but she didn't turn away. She gave her son a piece of paper.

'Keep this,' she told him. 'Look at it when you are ill. Take the things on it and you will feel better. Now please be careful!'

◆

Nothing happened between his home at Tarbes and the town of Meung, on the road to Paris, so d'Artagnan didn't have to use his sword.

At Meung, d'Artagnan stopped at the door of the biggest inn. He waited outside with his horse, and he looked round him. One of the windows of the inn was open, and inside d'Artagnan saw three men. They looked at d'Artagnan's horse and laughed.

'They are laughing at me,' d'Artagnan thought angrily. He called to them. 'What are you laughing at? When I see people laugh, I like to understand. Then I can laugh too.'

★ Gascon: a person from Gascony (Gascogne) in south-west France.

The most important man looked at d'Artagnan. 'I'm not talking to you,' he said.

When he heard this, d'Artagnan was more angry. He pulled his sword out, and he started to run into the inn.

But the innkeeper saw him. With three of his men, he attacked d'Artagnan. They had no swords, but the attack came from behind d'Artagnan. They hit him again and again on his head. He was on the ground before he could turn round.

They carried him into the kitchen. Then the innkeeper spoke to the important man.

'He is quiet now,' he said. 'He does not know anything. I do not think he is an important man. He hasn't much money and he only has one shirt. He has a letter with *To Monsieur de Tréville, Captain of the King's Musketeers* on it.

The innkeeper was right. D'Artagnan was very quiet. But he was a Gascon, and Gascons have hard heads. Five minutes later, he felt better and he was on his feet again. He went to the window and looked for the important man.

There, outside the inn, he saw him. He was by a big carriage with a young woman inside it. D'Artagnan could only see the young woman's head through the window of the carriage, but she was very beautiful. She was between twenty and twenty-two years old and she had large blue eyes, long hair and a beautiful face. She was talking quietly to the important man.

'So what does the Cardinal say?' she asked him.

'Go back to England now. When the Duke leaves London, tell the Cardinal.'

'Is that all?' asked the beautiful young woman.

'Open this box when you get to England.'

'All right. And what do you have to do?'

'I am going back to Paris.'

'No, you are not!' shouted d'Artagnan, and he ran out of the inn.

She had large blue eyes, long hair and a beautiful face.

The man's hand went to his sword, but the young woman in the carriage said, 'Remember the Cardinal's words!'

'The Cardinal,' thought d'Artagnan.

'You are right, Milady*,' said the man. 'We cannot wait.' He jumped on his horse, and the carriage driver started his horses. The carriage went one way, and the important man went the other way.

D'Artagnan started to run after him, but his head hurt. He fell down in the street.

'He will be here for a long time now,' said the innkeeper.

◆

He was wrong. D'Artagnan was up at five o'clock the next morning. He went down to the kitchen with his mother's piece of paper, and he found the right things. So, with his mother's help, d'Artagnan was nearly well again in the evening.

'Now,' he said to the innkeeper, 'where's my letter?'

'The other man took it from you yesterday,' the innkeeper answered. But he didn't really know the answer to d'Artagnan's question.

Chapter 2   The King's Musketeers

D'Artagnan found a room in Paris, and then he went to look for Monsieur de Tréville.

The captain of King Louis XIII's musketeers was easy to find. Everybody in the city knew him and his musketeers. The musketeers were nearly all men of good family. You could see them everywhere. They pushed past people. They shouted and

* Milady: the French name for an important English woman.

4

made a lot of noise. They were loud and angry, but they were ready to give their lives for the King.

The most important man in France at the time was not the King; it was Cardinal Richelieu. The Cardinal also had guards. Each man wanted the strongest and the best guards. Monsieur de Tréville's men often pushed the Cardinal's guards in the street and then a fight began. The King and the Cardinal knew about the fights. The King was always happy when some of his musketeers were in a fight and won. The Cardinal was happy when his guards won.

◆

When d'Artagnan arrived at Monsieur de Tréville's house, he found a large number of musketeers there. They played a game on the stairs with their swords, and he watched. When one man hurt another musketeer, they all laughed loudly.

D'Artagnan asked for Monsieur de Tréville. Then he stood and waited. He looked round at the other men there. One very tall musketeer had a fine sword, and he talked about it loudly all the time.

'No, Porthos,' another musketeer said. 'You did not buy that sword with the money from your father. The woman at the Porte St Honoré gave it to you last Sunday.'

'I tell you, I did pay for it. Is that not right, Aramis?'

Aramis was quite different from his friend. He was young – perhaps twenty-three – with dark eyes and a kind face.

He spoke very little. 'Yes,' he said quietly.

The door to de Tréville's room opened, and a man called out, 'Monsieur de Tréville will see Monsieur d'Artagnan.'

D'Artagnan went into the room. He was happy when the great man gave him his hand.

'I will talk to you in a minute,' said de Tréville. 'I have to do something now.' And he called out, 'Athos! Porthos! Aramis!'

Two musketeers came in.

'Where is Athos?' asked de Tréville.

'Athos is ill, sir, very ill,' said Aramis.

'Ill? What is wrong with him? Did somebody hurt him? Was there really a fight between six of the King's musketeers and six of the Cardinal's guards? You lost? That is bad – very bad! What is wrong with the musketeers?'

Porthos was angry. 'We did not see them. Before we could take out our swords, two of our men were dead. They hurt Athos badly. You know Athos well. He tried to get up, but he fell back. We fought, but they were six to three. Aramis broke his sword, but he took a sword from one of the Cardinal's men. He began to fight again. We did not run away.'

Then a man came to the door. He was a fine man, but he looked very ill. His face was white.

'Athos!' cried de Tréville and the two musketeers.

'You sent for me, sir,' said Athos – and fell to the floor.

'A doctor! Call a doctor!' said de Tréville. 'The King's doctor. The best doctor in Paris. Now!'

Porthos and Aramis ran out of the room and came back with a doctor. They took Athos away.

D'Artagnan was face to face with de Tréville.

'I am sorry about that,' said the great man. 'What can I do for you?'

'Sir,' said d'Artagnan, 'I had a letter . . .'

'It is all right. I know about you. Tell me – what can I do?'

'Sir, I came here because I wanted to be one of your musketeers. But I know now that only the best men can be musketeers.'

'Yes,' said de Tréville. 'First a man has to do well in one of the other companies.'

D'Artagnan was near a window. Suddenly he cried, 'There he is! He will not get away this time!' And he ran out of the room.

Chapter 3   Three Fights in a Day!

D'Artagnan ran from the room because he saw the man from Meung through the window. He ran to the stairs, and into another man in front of him. His head hit the other man's arm.

'I am sorry!' said d'Artagnan. 'I have to be quick.' He turned to the stairs again.

A strong hand on his arm stopped him. It was Athos.

'You have to be quick?' said the musketeer. 'So you run into me. Then you think that "sorry" makes everything all right? It does not. We do things differently here. Are you from the country?'

D'Artagnan wanted to go downstairs, but he wasn't happy.

'Listen, sir,' he said. 'I *am* from the country, but you cannot speak to me in that way!'

'Oh, can't I?'

'No! You cannot!' cried d'Artagnan. 'I cannot stop now, but. . .'

'Perhaps you cannot stop now, sir, but you can find me later.'

'Where can I find you?'

'Behind the church.'

'At what time?'

'About midday.'

'Midday? Right! I will be there.'

'And do not be late. I want to have your ears before a quarter past twelve.'

'Right!' said d'Artagnan. And he started to run again. He really wanted to catch the man from Meung.

Porthos was by the street door, but d'Artagnan didn't see him. He pushed against him.

'I am sorry,' said d'Artagnan, 'but I have to catch somebody.'

'Perhaps you do have to catch somebody,' said the big man. 'But do not push musketeers, or somebody will hurt you.'

'Hurt me!' cried d'Artagnan. 'No man is going to hurt me!'

'At one o'clock, then, behind the Luxembourg.'

'At one o'clock! Right!' shouted d'Artagnan.

D'Artagnan ran outside as fast as he could. He looked for the man from Meung, but he couldn't see him anywhere.

'I will find him,' d'Artagnan thought, and he began to walk home. 'I have to fight two men. I will have to be careful now. I cannot fight any more men!'

A minute or two later, d'Artagnan saw Aramis with three of the King's guards. D'Artagnan went closer. A handkerchief fell, and Aramis put his foot on it.

'Your handkerchief, sir,' said d'Artagnan, and he tried to give it to Aramis. It was a very beautiful woman's handkerchief.

'Ho, ho!' cried a guard. 'She likes you, so she is giving you one of her handkerchiefs, Aramis!'

Aramis looked angry and began to walk away.

'Your handkerchief,' said d'Artagnan. He tried again to give it to the musketeer.

'Young Gascon,' said Aramis angrily, 'it is not my handkerchief.'

'I saw it fall.'

'So, you think I am wrong?'

'Yes, I do.' And d'Artagnan's hand went to his sword.

'Not here,' Aramis said. 'We cannot fight here. The Cardinal's guards are everywhere round here. Meet me at two o'clock at Monsieur de Tréville's house. I will take you to a nice quiet place from there.'

'Right!' said d'Artagnan.

He began to walk to the church. 'Now I am going to have three fights,' he thought. 'But when somebody kills me, he will be a musketeer.'

Chapter 4   The Cardinal's Guards

When d'Artagnan arrived at the church, Athos was there before him. Athos wasn't well.

He said, 'My friends are not here, but they will be here in a minute or two. Then we can start.'

'I have no friends here, sir,' d'Artagnan answered. 'I do not know anybody in Paris. I only know Monsieur de Tréville because my father gave me a letter for him.'

'Oh!' said Athos. 'That is bad. And you are very young. People will be angry with me when I kill you. They will think the fight was wrong. You have to have a friend here.'

'It is not really wrong,' said d'Artagnon. 'You are not strong because you are ill. Listen, I can give you something and you will get better quickly. My mother told me about it and it worked for me. It really is wonderful. You will be better in three days. Let's wait three days and have our fight then.'

D'Artagnan really wanted to help him, and Athos knew that. It was not because he didn't want to fight.

'That is kind of you,' said Athos. 'I will not take your help, but you are a good man. Where are my friends? Why are they not here?'

'Perhaps you have not got much time,' said d'Artagnan. 'Perhaps you would like to kill me as quickly as possible. We can start without them.'

'I like you,' answered Athos. 'Perhaps you will not die. Then I hope that we can be friends. Ah, here is one of my friends now!'

'What!' cried d'Artagnan. 'Is Monsieur Porthos one of your friends?'

'Yes. And there is my other friend.'

'What! Is Monsieur Aramis your other friend?'

'Yes, he is. There are always three of us. Everybody calls us the three musketeers.'

Athos looked at d'Artagnan and said to his friends, 'I am going to fight this man.'

'But I am going to fight him too,' cried Porthos.

'Yes,' said d'Artagnan. 'But at one o'clock.'

'And me?' asked Aramis.

'At two o'clock,' said d'Artagnan.

'Well, we can start now,' said Athos. 'When you are ready.'

D'Artagnan and Athos took out their swords. But suddenly five of the Cardinal's guards arrived with Monsieur de Jussac.

'The Cardinal's guards!' cried Porthos and Aramis. 'Put your swords away quickly.'

But it was too late.

'Stop fighting, musketeers,' said de Jussac. 'You know that you cannot fight. Give us your swords and come with us.'

'Sir,' said Aramis, 'only Monsieur de Tréville can stop us. Please go away.'

'You will come with us,' said de Jussac angrily.

Athos spoke very quietly. Only his friends and d'Artagnan could hear him.

'There are five of them and only three of us. We will lose again, and then we cannot go back to the Captain. We will have to die here.'

'Excuse me!' said d'Artagnan. 'Monsieur Athos says that there are only three of us. I think that we are four.'

The three musketeers looked at him. He was very young, but he was also quite strong.

'All right. And thank you,' said Athos. 'What is your name, young man?'

'D'Artagnan.'

'Right. We are Athos, Porthos, Aramis, and d'Artagnan now!'

The fight started. Athos fought Cahusac, one of the Cardinal's best swordsmen. Porthos fought Bicarat, and Aramis fought two of the guards. D'Artagnan was face to face with de Jussac.

The fight started.

De Jussac usually won his fights. He hoped to kill the young man quickly. Then he could help his friends. But the young man moved very quickly. De Jussac was angry. How could a young nobody fight the great de Jussac? Because he was angry, de Jussac began to do stupid things. He pushed his sword at the younger man. In that way he usually killed his man. But d'Artagnan turned de Jussac's sword away with his sword. It came under de Jussac's arm and went through him. De Jussac fell to the ground.

Aramis killed one of his two men, and turned to fight the other guard. Porthos hurt Bicarat and Bicarat hurt Porthos. But they enjoyed the fight. Athos fought well, but he was ill. He looked at d'Artagnan, and the young man ran to him.

D'Artagnan began to fight Cahusac, and Cahusac's sword flew out of his hand.

Aramis killed his second man, and Porthos could kill Bicarat at any time.

De Jussac was on the ground, but now he sat up.

'Stop!' he called to Bicarat.

The fight was at an end. The three musketeers and d'Artagnan carried the swords of the five Cardinal's guards to de Tréville. They were very happy.

Chapter 5   The Queen's Diamonds

Monsieur de Tréville was also very happy with his three musketeers and their new friend, d'Artagnan. He told the King about the fight, and the King was excited too.

'Talk to Monsieur des Essarts. He will have to find a place in his guards for this young Gascon,' said the King.

And so d'Artagnan was now one of the King's guards.

'Do well,' said de Tréville, 'and you can be one of the King's musketeers in a year or two.'

D'Artagnan was happy because now he had three friends in the musketeers – Athos, Porthos and Aramis.

The four men had many exciting times, many fights, and many laughs. Each man was always ready to help the others: 'One for all, all for one!'

◆

D'Artagnan was often a guard in the Queen's rooms. One of the Queen's women, Constance Bonacieux, was young and very pretty. D'Artagnan fell in love with her when he first saw her. She fell in love with him too. She told him about the Queen.

'The Queen is not happy,' she said. 'The King thinks that she is in love with the Duke of Buckingham. He is a very important man in England. The Cardinal hates the Queen and he wants the King to hate her too.'

The Queen liked the Duke of Buckingham very much, and she gave him some very fine diamond pins. She had them because the King gave them to her.

The Cardinal learned about the diamonds. He had people everywhere. They listened and told him everything. The Cardinal sent a woman, Milady, to England. She had to take some or all of the diamond pins from the Duke of Buckingham.

A letter came to the Cardinal from England.

I have got them. But I cannot leave London without more money. Send me some money, and I will be in Paris in five days.

The Cardinal spoke to the King. 'There is going to be a great dinner and dance here in Paris in twelve days' time. We would like you and the Queen to be there.'

'Oh, good!' said the King. He loved dances.

Then the Cardinal said: 'Please ask the Queen to wear her wonderful diamond pins.'

The next day, the King spoke to the Queen about the dance and about the diamonds.

'Did the Cardinal plan the dinner and the dance?' the Queen asked.

'Yes.'

'And I have to wear the diamonds? That was the Cardinal's idea too?'

'Yes – yes, it was.'

When the King went back to his rooms, the Queen started to cry. 'What can I do?' she thought. 'The Cardinal knows everything. The King does not know now, but he will. The Cardinal will tell him. I cannot send anybody to Buckingham. The Cardinal will stop them.'

'I think I can help,' said Constance Bonacieux. 'Are you unhappy about the diamond pins? Is that the problem? The Duke of Buckingham has them and we have to get them back?'

The Queen looked at the pretty face. Constance's eyes were kind, and the Queen thought, 'Constance wants to help me. She does not work for the Cardinal.'

'Yes,' the Queen said, 'but how can we get them back?'

'We will have to send somebody to the Duke.'

'Who? Who will go? And I will have to send a letter. But I cannot do that. The Cardinal will find it and that will be the end of me. The King will send me away.'

Constance said, 'I know somebody. He will take the letter to England, and he will not tell the Cardinal.'

Chapter 6   To England for the Queen

Constance Bonacieux, of course, gave the Queen's letter to d'Artagnan.

D'Artagnan was very happy. 'Constance loves me!' he thought. 'I will leave now,' he cried.

'The King will send me away.'

'Here is some money for your journey,' she said, and she gave him a bag of money.

D'Artagnan went to de Tréville and said, 'I have to do something for the Queen. It is important for her good name, and perhaps for her life.'

De Tréville said, 'What do you want from me? Tell me. I will help.'

'Please ask Monsieur des Essarts to give me fourteen days. I will have to go away for that time.'

'Where are you going? Can you tell me?'

'To London.'

'Who wants to stop you?'

'The Cardinal, I think.'

'I will send your three friends with you. We will say that Athos is ill. Porthos and Aramis have to help him, so they are going too. I will give you some permits. The permits will say that they have to go to the sea. It will be good for Athos there.'

'Thank you, sir.'

When their permits came from de Tréville, the three musketeers wanted to know everything.

'What is this journey for?' asked Porthos.

'We are going to London,' d'Artagnan told them. 'But I cannot tell you much. I have to take a letter to London. It is here in my bag. The Cardinal will try to stop me, and perhaps his men will kill me. Then one of you will have to take the letter. One of us has to get to London with the letter.'

◆

At two o'clock in the morning the four friends left Paris. They arrived at Chantilly at eight o'clock in the morning, and had breakfast at an inn. But when they were ready to leave, a man spoke to Porthos. 'Drink to the Cardinal,' he said.

Porthos did this, and then he asked the other man to drink to the King. The man took out his sword, and cried, 'I know no king, only the Cardinal!'

'I know that you have to fight this man,' Athos said to Porthos. 'That is all right. We will wait for you for two hours at Beauvais.'

They waited at Beauvais, but Porthos did not come.

'There are only three of us now,' said Athos.

After only a short time on the road they had to go past some trees. Suddenly, eight men with muskets attacked them from the trees. One of them hit Aramis and hurt him badly.

'We cannot stop and fight them,' cried d'Artagnan. 'There is no time.'

But at Crèvecoeur, Athos and d'Artagnan had to leave Aramis at an inn.

The two men arrived at Amiens at midnight and stopped at another inn. In the morning d'Artagnan found the horses and Athos paid the innkeeper. Then d'Artagnan saw four or five men with swords and guns. The men ran into the inn. There was a noise, and then Athos shouted, 'They have got me! Get away, quickly!'

D'Artagnan had to leave him there.

When he was nearly in Calais, his horse fell. After that, he had to walk.

D'Artagnan arrived in Calais and found the ships. He listened to the captain of one of the ships. The captain was with another man.

'I would like to take you across to England,' the captain said. 'But from this morning, nobody can go on a ship without a permit from the Cardinal.'

'I have got a permit,' the man said. 'Here it is.'

'All right, Monsieur le Comte★. Take it to the office. The man there will put his name on it and then we can go. The office is in that street there.'

★ Comte: the French word for a count, an important man in France at that time.

The man started to walk quickly. D'Artagnan ran after him and stopped him in the quiet street.

'Are you going somewhere?' he asked.

'Yes, I am. Get out of my way.'

'Of course. But I want your permit from the Cardinal.'

The man took out his sword and tried to kill d'Artagnan. But d'Artagnan was too quick for him. He took out his sword and with it he turned the other man's sword away. D'Artagnan's sword went through the man, and he fell to the ground.

D'Artagnan found the Cardinal's permit. It was for the 'Comte de Wardes'. He took it to the office. The man there didn't know the Comte de Wardes, so he put his name on the permit. Then d'Artagnan went back to the ship.

He paid the captain some money, and in a short time he was at sea, on his way to England.

D'Artagnan knew no English, but he found somebody at Dover. This man could speak French, and he helped d'Artagnan to get a horse. After that, he showed him the right road for London.

When d'Artagnan arrived there, he wrote the Duke of Buckingham's name on a piece of paper. Then he showed it to people. Everybody knew the great man's house.

Chapter 7   The Duke of Buckingham

'A letter for the Duke?' said a man at the door. 'Give it to me.'

'No,' said d'Artagnan. 'I have to give it to the Duke.'

'A letter for the Duke?' said a man inside the house. 'I will take it to him.'

'No,' said d'Artagnan.

In the end he saw the Duke.

'What do you have to tell me?' asked the Duke. 'Is something wrong? Is it the Queen?'

And from the Duke's words, d'Artagnan knew. He loved the Queen. D'Artagnan put his hand inside his coat and pulled out the Queen's letter.

'Read this,' he said.

The Duke read the letter and then went quickly to a box. He took out the wonderful diamond pins.

'These are the Queen's diamonds,' he said. 'She gave them to me, but now she wants them again. She has to have them as quickly as possible.'

He looked again at the diamonds and suddenly he shouted, 'Oh no! There were twelve pins, but now there are only ten! Two are not here.'

'Not here?' said d'Artagnan.

'Yes, look. But who did it? Let me think. Ah, yes, I remember now. I wore the diamonds at a dinner and Lady de Winter was there. She spoke to me two or three times, and that was strange. She works for the Cardinal, and she does not like me. So she has two of the diamond pins. That is bad, but we can do something about it. I will have to buy two more diamond pins, and they will have to look the same.'

So the Duke paid a man, and the man made two more diamond pins.

◆

Two days later, d'Artagnan started on his journey back to Paris.

The Duke of Buckingham's men worked hard. A ship took d'Artagnan to the small French town of St Valéry. He found a very fine horse there, and there were three other horses at inns on the road to Paris. The journey from St Valéry to Paris was about twelve hours.

When he arrived in Paris, d'Artagnan went to de Tréville's house. De Tréville asked no questions.

'You can sleep here tonight,' he said.

Chapter 8   The Great Dinner

The next day, everybody in Paris was excited about the dinner and dance. When the King arrived, the great and rich men and women of Paris were there. The King didn't look happy.

The Queen arrived five minutes later. She, too, looked sad – or was she only tired?

The Cardinal met her. There were no diamonds on her! Suddenly he looked really happy. He spoke to the King.

'Ask the Queen about her diamonds. You remember – you wanted her to wear them.'

The King looked very angry. He went to the Queen and said: 'Why aren't you wearing your diamonds?'

'I did not want to lose them on the way here, but I will put them on now.'

'Please do that.' The King left her, and the Queen went to another room.

The Cardinal gave the King a box. There were two diamond pins in it.

'What does this mean?' the King asked.

'The Queen says that she has her diamonds. I do not think that she has. Look at her when she comes back. How many pins is she wearing? Only ten, I think. Ask her about the other two.'

The King looked at the Cardinal. He wanted to ask more questions. But suddenly the Queen was there again. She had a different dress now, and she looked very beautiful. On her dress there were twelve diamond pins.

The Cardinal's face went dark red, and he looked angry and afraid. The Queen had the diamonds – but were there twelve or only ten?

The King walked across to his wife.

'Thank you,' he said. 'You put the diamonds on very quickly. But did you not lose two pins? Here they are.' He gave the Queen the Cardinal's two pins.

The Cardinal looked angry and afraid.

'I do not understand,' said the Queen. 'Are you giving me two more diamond pins? Then I will have fourteen!'

The King looked at the pins on her dress. Twelve! He turned and called the Cardinal to him. He was very, very angry. Everybody knew that, but nobody could hear his words to the Cardinal.

Was that a smile on the Queen's face?

◆

Later that night, d'Artagnan was on guard at the Queen's rooms.

'Please come with me. Be very quiet.' It was Constance Bonacieux. She took him into a small dark room next to a much bigger room. He could hear somebody in the bigger room.

Constance left him. After a minute, the door opened a little, and d'Artagnan saw an arm – a very beautiful arm.

He took the lovely white hand. It was the Queen's hand, and she pushed something into his hand. Then the arm went back through the door.

After a time Constance came and took him back into the light. D'Artagnan opened his hand. In it was a beautiful diamond.

Chapter 9   D'Artagnan's Friends

D'Artagnan left Paris again, because he wanted to find his friends. At Chantilly, the innkeeper was happy to see him.

'Yes,' he said, 'your friend is here. He is nearly better. Well – he lost the fight. But he does not want anybody to know that.'

'Lost the fight? What fight? You will have to tell me now.'

'The fight finished very quickly. The other man's sword went into Monsieur Porthos before he could do anything. Then the man asked Monsieur Porthos his name. When he heard it, he said: "What! Not d'Artagnan?" He helped Monsieur Porthos to his feet and then he left my inn.'

D'Artagnan went up and found his friend. The big man was in bed, but he had a plate of food and a bottle of wine.

'Oh, there you are!' he said. 'Do you know about the fight?'

'No. What happened? The innkeeper told me your room number, and here I am. We waited for you at Beauvais but you did not come.'

'Oh, I taught a man to use a sword, but I caught my foot on something. When I fell, I hurt my leg badly.'

'And the other man?'

'Oh, he left.'

D'Artagnan asked, 'Will you be all right here? I have to go and look for the other musketeers.'

'You go and find them,' said Porthos. 'I will be fine.' He looked happily at his food and his bottle.

◆

At Crèvecoeur, d'Artagnan went to the inn. The innkeeper there was a woman.

'Can you tell me about my friend?' he asked her. 'I left him here last week.'

'A fine young man of about twenty-five? He is here now. A really nice man!'

'Good. I will go and see him.'

'I do not think you can see him now, sir. Two important men from the church are with him.'

'Why?' cried d'Artagnan. 'Is he very ill? Is he dying?'

'No, sir. He is better. But he wants to be a man of the Church.'

D'Artagnan ran to Aramis's room. Aramis looked round when the door opened.

'Ah!' he said, but he was not really excited. 'D'Artagnan!'

'Are you coming back to Paris with me?' asked d'Artagnan.

'Well, no. I am going to go into the Church. My two friends here are going to help me.'

'Oh!' said d'Artagnan. He thought for a minute. 'So you will not want the letter?'

'What letter?'

'It came for you when you were away. It is from Tours, and it has the same name on it as that handkerchief.'

'Where is it?' cried Aramis.

'I have it here somewhere . . .' he laughed.

Aramis cried, 'Find it! Find it!'

D'Artagnan found the letter quite easily. Aramis opened it quickly and read it.

'Oh, d'Artagnan! She loves me! Oh, I am very happy!' He took d'Artagnan by the hand, and they danced round the two men from the Church.

'Now we have to find Athos,' said d'Artagnan. But when Aramis climbed on his horse, he cried out.

'You start back slowly to Paris,' said d'Artagnan, 'and I will find Athos.'

D'Artagnan liked Athos the best of the three musketeers. Athos was quiet and intelligent, but he enjoyed laughing with his friends.

At Amiens, d'Artagnan pushed his way into the noisy inn. 'Where is my friend? I left him here,' he shouted at the innkeeper.

'I did not do anything. The men — about eight of them — attacked him. He killed two of them with his musket, and another with his sword . . .'

'Where is he?'

'He is in the wine cupboard, sir. He went in and shut the door. Then he put heavy boxes behind it.'

'What!' shouted d'Artagnan. 'Is he in there now?'

'Yes, sir, yes! He will not come out. We want to get in there for more wine.'

'Where is the door?' The man took him to it. 'Athos!' called d'Artagnan. 'You can come out now. There is only me here.'

D'Artagnan could hear noises in the cupboard – Athos moved the heavy boxes. Then the door opened and Athos came out. He had a bottle under each arm.

The innkeeper brought food to them and then went to the cupboard. 'My wine! My food! Where is it?' he cried.

D'Artagnan told Athos about Porthos and Aramis.

'I found Porthos in bed with a bad leg,' he said. 'And then I found Aramis with two men from the Church.'

'And what happened to you?' asked Athos.

'I am in love with Constance.'

'That is bad,' said Athos.

'But you always say that. You know nothing about love.'

So then Athos told d'Artagnan about his 'friend'. This 'friend' met a very beautiful girl. She was beautiful and very intelligent. He married her, and for months he was very happy. But then he began to learn things about her. She was not very kind to people, and Athos's 'friend' did not like this. Then he learned more. She was a bad woman in every way.

'So I will never fall in love again. That woman is Lady de Winter – they call her "Milady".'

D'Artagnan understood. The 'friend' in Athos's story was not really a friend at all. The story was about Athos, and Milady was his wife!

Chapter 10   Milady's Plans

The Huguenots* had the city of La Rochelle. King Louis XIII and Cardinal Richelieu wanted to take it back, so they sent an army there. The Cardinal went first with the army, and the King followed with his musketeers and guards.

* Huguenots: French Protestants. Most French people were Catholics.

On their way to La Rochelle, Athos, Porthos and Aramis stopped at an inn near the city. They heard a lot of noise at the top of the stairs, and the innkeeper asked for their help.

'There is a woman up there,' he said, 'and three men are trying to get into her room.'

The three musketeers quickly sent the three men away. Then they had a drink and left. Suddenly they saw two men on horses. The men came nearer and then stopped.

Athos called: 'Who is there?'

One of the men called back: 'Who are you?'

'That is not an answer,' called Athos. 'I said "Who is there?" Answer now or you will be sorry.'

'I will not be sorry. Why are you here at this time of night?'

He was an important man. Athos could hear that.

'We are King's Musketeers,' he said.

'Your name?' said the other man. He had his hand over his face.

'Show us your face,' said Athos.

The man took his hand away and showed his face. It was the Cardinal.

'Your name?' the Cardinal said again.

'Athos.'

'So the two men with you are Porthos and Aramis?'

'Yes, sir.'

'Then please follow me. But what are you doing here?'

Athos told him about the fight at the inn. 'The three men wanted to push their way into the woman's room,' he said.

'This woman,' said the Cardinal, 'was she young and pretty?'

'We did not see her, sir,' Athos answered.

'Oh, good. Well, I am on my way to the inn now. Come with me.'

At the inn the Cardinal spoke to the innkeeper. 'Show these men to a room,' he said. 'They can wait there.'

Porthos and Aramis started to play a game of cards, but Athos couldn't sit quietly. He walked round the room. Then he stopped and stood near the fireplace. He could hear people in the room above. He heard the Cardinal: 'This is very important, Milady. We have to do it right.'

'Milady!' Athos said very quietly. Porthos and Aramis stopped playing and went to him.

'What can I do for you now, sir?' said a woman.

When he heard her, Athos's face went white.

The Cardinal said, 'A ship is waiting for you at the mouth of the Charente river. Go to London again. When you get there, visit the Duke of Buckingham.'

Milady said, 'But he will know about the diamond pins. He will not listen to me.'

'This time you are going to speak to him openly for me and for France. I know that he is planning to send ships and men to the Protestants at La Rochelle. I do not want him to send them. Say that I know about his love for the Queen. I know that he meets her. Say that I will tell the King and everybody.'

'Perhaps that will not stop him,' Milady answered.

'Then you know that he has to die.'

Milady said nothing for a minute, then: 'All right, sir. I understand. I will do that for you. Now will you do something for me? I want some people to die too.'

'Who?'

'Constance Bonacieux and d'Artagnan.'

The Cardinal did not understand. 'Why d'Artagnan? He is a fine man.'

'Yes, but dangerous. He fought your guards with the King's musketeers and won. He killed my lover, the Comte de Wardes. He helped the Queen with the diamond pins ...'

'All right. Give me a pen and paper,' said the Cardinal.

◆

When the Cardinal came down again, Athos said to him, 'When we leave here, please let me go before you, sir. Porthos and Aramis will go with you. Then we can guard you well.'

'Yes,' said the Cardinal. 'Do that.'

So Athos left quickly, but a little way down the road he turned into the trees. He waited, and the Cardinal and the men with him went past. Then he went quickly back to the inn.

Milady was afraid when she saw the musketeer. Then he came nearer, and her face went white.

'You know me, then,' said Athos.

'You are not dead!'

'No. I am not dead – but your second husband is. Then de Winter married you, and he is dead too. You killed them for their money.'

'What do you want?'

'The Cardinal wrote a permit for you. Give it to me.'

She saw the gun in his hand, and she gave him the piece of paper. Athos opened it and read:

The person with this letter in his hand
is helping me and France.
3 December 1627   Richelieu

Chapter 11   Breakfast at the Bastion

'We have to talk.'

D'Artagnan looked at Athos's face. It was important.

'We can go to the Parpaillot inn for breakfast,' he said. 'The walls there will be thicker than here.'

So the four friends went to the inn. But there were a lot of other people there too. King's guards, the Cardinal's guards, musketeers, Swiss guards and other men came in and out.

Athos said, 'This is not a good place. We will have to wait. D'Artagnan, tell us about your night and we will tell you about ours later.'

De Busigny, a guard from their company, was near them. He heard Athos's last words and said, 'Yes, did you have a fight at La Rochelle last night?'

'Did you not attack a bastion?' asked a Swiss guard.

'Yes, we took the St Gervais bastion,' answered d'Artagnan, 'and we killed some guards there.'

Suddenly Athos said, 'Do you want to put your money on something?'

'On what?' asked de Busigny.

'I say that I and my three friends are going to have breakfast in the St Gervais bastion. We will stay there for one hour.'

'And I say that you cannot do it,' said de Busigny. 'They will attack you. How much money are you putting on it?'

'There are four of us and four of you. Perhaps a very good dinner for eight people? The losers will pay for the dinner. What do you say?'

'Very good,' said de Busigny and the other men.

'Your breakfast is ready,' the innkeeper called.

'We will take it with us,' said Athos.

When they left the inn, d'Artagnan asked, 'What is this about?'

Athos said, 'We have to make some important plans. We could not talk at the inn.'

◆

They arrived at the bastion, and the four friends looked back at the French army. Two or three hundred men were there. De Busigny and his three friends were with them.

Athos took his hat, put it on the end of his sword, and pushed it high above his head. The French army shouted happily when they saw that.

There were twelve or more dead men in the bastion.

'Now,' said Athos, 'let's get the guns and musket balls from these dead men. We can talk at the same time. These dead men are not listening to us. How many muskets are there?'

'Twelve,' said Aramis. 'And about a hundred musket balls.'

'Good,' said Athos. 'Let's get the guns. Then we will eat.'

'But what do you want to tell us?' d'Artagnan asked.

'Well, I saw Milady last night.'

'What! You saw your . . .'

Athos put up his hand. 'Be careful. The others do not know as much as you do. Milady has a permit from the Cardinal. She wants to kill you, d'Artagnan.'

Chapter 12   Attack!

Aramis looked out at La Rochelle. 'About twenty men are coming, but some of them are workmen,' he said. 'They are going to build the walls again.'

'Where are they?' asked Athos.

'About 500 metres away.'

'Good. We can finish this bottle of wine.'

When there was no more wine in the bottle, Athos stood up.

'Let's send them away,' he said. Then he called, 'My good men, some friends and I are having breakfast in this bastion. Please go away and come back later.'

'They are going to attack!' cried d'Artagnan.

'I know.' said Athos. 'But they are not very good, so they will not hit us.'

Four musket balls hit the bastion all round Athos, but they did not hit him. The four friends took up their muskets. Three of the attackers fell dead, and the musketeers hurt another man. The workmen ran back to the town.

'Please go away and come back later.'

'Let's finish our breakfast,' said Athos, 'but one of us will have to watch for an attack. We will now tell d'Artagnan about last night.'

Next, about twenty-five men came from La Rochelle to the bastion.

'There are a lot of them,' said Porthos. 'Can we stop them?'

'We have to,' said Athos. 'We have to finish breakfast. Ten more minutes. We said an hour – remember? We will use all the muskets. Then we will push this wall down on top of them.'

The musketeers fought well, and ten men from La Rochelle died. The other men started to climb up the bastion, but the four friends pushed the wall down. It was weak from the attack the night before. The men below shouted loudly.

'Have we really killed all of them?' Aramis asked.

'No,' said Porthos. 'Four or five are going back to La Rochelle.'

'They will send half their army next time,' said d'Artagnan.

'Well, we will have to use *our* army,' said Athos. 'We can use these men.' And he pushed a dead man on to the inside wall of the bastion and put a musket by him. The other three laughed and did the same with the other dead men.

Then Athos said, 'Milady is Lady de Winter. She killed her husband, and he was a friend of the Duke of Buckingham. Milady is on her way to England now. We have to tell the Duke about this. Can we get a letter to him?'

'Yes,' said d'Artagnan. 'There is a man at St Valéry. He can take it to him.'

They were very happy with their little army of dead men.

'The men from La Rochelle will go more slowly when they see our army,' said Athos. 'And here they come!'

Large numbers of men from La Rochelle began to move nearer to the bastion. They came slowly and carefully.

'It's an hour now,' said Athos. 'We can go. Let's tell our friends first.'

The four friends stood high on the walls of the bastion. The men from La Rochelle tried to hit them, but they couldn't. The musket balls didn't come near them.

The French army watched. There were 2,000 men or more there now.

Athos, Porthos, Aramis and d'Artagnan walked back to their army. They laughed when they heard a sudden great noise from behind them.

'They are trying to kill the dead men,' said Aramis.

'Yes,' said Athos. 'And the dead men will not attack. So they will think it is a clever plan, and they will talk about it first. We have a lot of time.'

The three friends walked back slowly. The French army watched them and shouted loudly.

The Cardinal sent Houdinière, the captain of his guards. He asked the musketeers about the noise.

'What is happening?' the Cardinal asked, when Houdinière came back.

'Three musketeers and a guard had breakfast at the St Gervais bastion. And when they were there, they killed a lot of men from La Rochelle, sir.'

The Cardinal asked, 'What are the names of the musketeers?'

'Athos, Porthos and Aramis, sir.'

'Those three again! And the guard?'

'Monsieur d'Artagnan.'

'Him again!'

Chapter 13   The New Lieutenant

When Milady's ship arrived at Portsmouth, a young man climbed on to it from an English boat. He spoke to the captain and then said to Milady, 'Please come with me.'

33

He and his men took her to a room in a big house, and then they left. After a time, another man came in.

Milady looked at him. 'De Winter!' she cried. 'Oh, no!'

'Yes,' answered de Winter, 'your second husband's brother. You married him and then killed him. And your first husband was not dead. Now you have to die for that.'

◆

Houdinière, the captain of the Cardinal's guards, found Athos, Porthos, Aramis and d'Artagnan in an inn.

'Monsieur d'Artagnan, please come with me to the Cardinal now,' he said.

That night, when the Cardinal came back to his house, he found d'Artagnan and his three friends at his door.

D'Artagnan was without his sword, but the other three had swords and guns.

'Come with me, Monsieur d'Artagnan,' the Cardinal said.

'We will wait for you, d'Artagnan,' said Athos.

The Cardinal heard him and stopped for a minute. Then he went into the house and into his office without a word. D'Artagnan followed him.

They were the only two people in the room, and there was a table between them. The Cardinal said, 'Why are you here? Do you know?'

'No, sir. What did I do?'

'Better men than you lost their heads for these things,' said the Cardinal angrily.

'What things?' asked d'Artagnan quietly.

'You spoke to the Duke of Buckingham, and sent him a letter. You took and used a permit from me . . .'

'Yes, sir. A very bad woman told you these things. This woman married and killed two men. And her first husband was not dead.'

'What are you saying?' the Cardinal cried. 'Which woman are you talking about?'

'Lady de Winter – Milady!'

'I did not know about her husbands. Where is she now?'

'Dead, sir.'

'What!'

'She is dead.'

'Dead? You are saying that she is dead? Who killed her?'

'In a way, my friends and I did.'

The Cardinal looked at the young man, but d'Artagnan was not afraid.

'Then you will have to die,' he said. 'You were wrong to kill her.'

'But I have a piece of paper. It says that everything is all right,' d'Artagnan said.

'A piece of paper?'

'Yes, sir.'

'And who put his name on it? The King?'

'No,' answered d'Artagnan. 'It has your name on it.'

He pulled out the piece of paper and gave it to the Cardinal. It was Milady's permit from the Cardinal.

Richelieu read it:

The person with this letter in his hand
is helping me and France.
3 December 1627   Richelieu

He read it again carefully. He sat and thought for a minute or two. Then he threw away the piece of paper.

'Well,' d'Artagnan thought, 'I am not afraid to die.'

The Cardinal stood up slowly and walked to the table.

He wrote something on a piece of paper and put his name on it. Then he gave it to d'Artagnan.

'Take this paper. Look at it. There is no name on it, so you can write in the name.'

D'Artagnan looked at it quickly.

It was a paper for a new lieutenant in the musketeers! But there was no name on it.

The Cardinal said, 'You are a good man, d'Artagnan. Write your name on it. But remember – I gave it to you.' Then he called, 'Rochefort!'

The important man from Meung came in.

'Rochefort,' said the Cardinal. 'You see Monsieur d'Artagnan here. Well, now he is my friend. So, stop fighting. Give him your hand.'

That evening d'Artagnan visited Athos. He wanted to give the paper to him.

'No,' said Athos. 'The Cardinal wants you to be a lieutenant. You will be a good one.'

Next d'Artagnan visited Porthos. 'I want to give you something,' he said.

'What is that?' Porthos asked.

'This paper,' d'Artagnan answered. 'Write your name on it.'

Porthos looked at it and then gave it back to d'Artagnan.

'No,' he said. 'It is yours. You take it.'

So the young man visited Aramis.

'Thank you, but no,' said Aramis. 'You have it. You will do well in the army.'

D'Artagnan went back to Athos's rooms.

'The other two will not take the paper,' he said.

'Because it is for you,' Athos said. He took his pen, and on the paper he wrote the name 'd'Artagnan'.

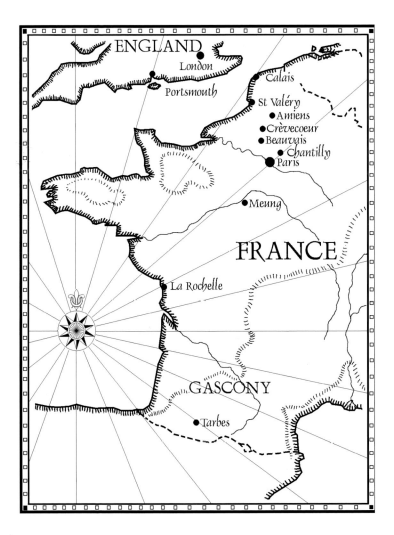

ACTIVITIES

Chapters 1–2

Before you read

1 Look at the picture on the front of this book. When and where do you think this story happens? Read the Introduction and find the answers.

2 Look at the Word List at the back of the book.

   a Find new words in your dictionary.

   b Which of these people was the most important at the time of the story? What do you think? Number them, 1 (the most important) to 6.

   duke   captain   innkeeper   guard   king   queen

While you read

3 Who:

   a gives d'Artagnan a sword?   ....

   b gives him a piece of paper?   ....

   c hits him on the head from behind?   ....

   d is sitting in a carriage?   ....

   e is going to take a box to England?   ....

   f does d'Artagnan want to fight?   ....

4 Name the person.

   a the captain of the King's musketeers   ....

   b the most important man in France   ....

   c a very tall man; he talks loudly   ....

   d a man with a kind face; he doesn't
   talk much   ....

   e a fine man; he looks ill   ....

After you read

5 Find the mistakes in these sentences.

   a D'Artagnan was born in Meung.

   b The men at the inn think d'Artagnan has a fine horse.

   c The important man and the woman are working for the Duke.

   d The important man is going to go to England.

   e The musketeers are very quiet and hate fighting.

   f D'Artagnan can be a musketeer now.

   g D'Artagnan sees the innkeeper from Meung out of the window.

6 Work with other students. You are Parisians. Many musketeers and guards live in your city. What do they do? What do you think of them? Talk about them.

Chapters 3–4

Before you read

7 Do you think d'Artagnan will make friends with Porthos, Aramis and Athos? Why (not)?

While you read

8 Make notes about the plans for d'Artagnan's fights.

Who	Where	When
		midday
	behind the Luxembourg	
Aramis		

9 The musketeers and d'Artagnan fight the Cardinal's guards. Finish the sentences with words on the right.

   a Cahusac is one of   with d'Artagnan.

   b De Jussac has a bad fight   the Cardinal's best swordsmen.

   c Porthos has a good fight   take five swords to de Tréville.

   d Aramis kills two of   with Bicarat.

   e The musketeers   the Cardinal's guards.

After you read

10 Aramis does not want to take the handkerchief from d'Artagnan. Why not, do you think? Discuss your ideas with another student.

11 D'Artagnan meets Athos at the church. Are these sentences right (✓) or wrong (✗)?

   a D'Artagnan has many friends in Paris.

   b Athos is weak and ill.

   c D'Artagnan says he can help Athos.

   d Athos wants to kill d'Artagnan as quickly as possible.

Chapters 5–6

Before you read

12 The year is 1630. You are going on a journey from Paris to London. How will you get there? What will you take? Where will you stay? What problems will you have? Discuss these questions with other students.

While you read

13 Write the names.

    a The King gave the diamond pins to the ....

    b The Queen gave the pins to the ....

    c The Cardinal wants .... to get the pins from the Duke.

    d The .... has to wear the pins to a dinner and dance.

    e .... has to take a letter about the pins to the Duke.

14 D'Artagnan goes from Paris to London. Where does he go first? Number the places, 1–7. Follow their journey on the map on page 37.

Amiens	,,,,,	Chantilly		London	.....
Dover	.....	Beauvais	.....	Calais	.....
Crèvecoeur	.....				

After you read

15 D'Artagnan takes the Queen's letter to the Duke. What does the letter say, do you think? Write it with another student.

16 Why don't the musketeers go to England with d'Artagnan? Finish these sentences.

    a Porthos stays in Chantilly because ... .

    b Aramis stays in Crèvecoeur because ... .

    c Athos stays in Amiens because ... .

Chapters 7–9

Before you read

17 Work with another student. Have this conversation.

> *Student A:* You are d'Artagnan. You are in London and looking for the Duke's house. Ask for help. (Your English is very bad!)
>
> *Student B:* You are a Londoner, in a London street. Try to help d'Artagnan.

18 Milady has some or all of the pins. What will the Duke do, do you think? Will the Queen get the pins before the dance?

While you read

19 Write numbers in these sentences.

    a There are only .... pins in the Duke's box.

    b Milady (Lady de Winter) has .... of the pins.

    c The Duke buys .... more pins.

    d The Queen is wearing .... pins at the beginning of the evening.

    e Later, she puts on .... pins.

    f The Cardinal shows the King .... pins in a box.

    g At the end of the evening, the Queen has .... pins!

20 Which is the right answer?

    a Who gives d'Artagnan a diamond?

        Constance   the Queen

    b Who won the fight at the inn at Chantilly?

        Porthos   the Cardinal's man

    c What is Aramis going to do?

        go into the Church   stay with his friends

    d Who is Athos's wife?

        Milady   Constance

After you read

21 Answer these questions.

    a Who is cleverer – the Cardinal, or the Queen and the Duke?

    b Why does the Cardinal's man attack Porthos?

    c Why does Aramis want to go into the Church?

    d What did Athos learn about his wife after he married her?

Chapters 10–11

Before you read

22 D'Artagnan and the three musketeers are good friends now. Can you think of another book or film about three or four friends? Tell other students about it.

While you read

23 Write *loves* or *hates* in the sentences.

    a The King .... the Huguenots.

    b The Duke of Buckingham .... the Queen.

    c Milady .... Constance and d'Artagnan.

    d Athos .... Milady.

24 Write these words in the sentences.

    in in for for to

    The musketeers are going to have breakfast and talk ..... the St Gervais bastion. They are going to stay there ..... one hour. De Busigny thinks that the Huguenots will attack them ..... the bastion. He thinks they will have to run back ..... the inn. Then the musketeers will have to buy dinner ..... de Busigny and his friends.

After you read

25 Who:

    a do the musketeers help at the inn?

    b do the musketeers meet when they leave the inn?

    c is going to help the Huguenots with ships and men?

    d wants d'Artagnan and Constance to die?

    e thinks that Athos is dead?

    f are happy when the musketeers are in the bastion?

26 Why does Athos really take the other musketeers to the bastion?

Chapters 12–13

Before you read

27 Who do you think will pay for the dinner – the musketeers, or de Busigny and his men? Why?

While you read

28 Which happens first? Number the sentences, 1–6.

    a About twenty-five men come from La Rochelle.   .....

    b A lot of men from La Rochelle move slowly to the bastion. .....

    c The four friends walk back to their army.   .....

    d The musketeers kill most of them.   .....

    e The musketeers kill three men.   .....

    f Twenty men come to the bastion from La Rochelle.   .....

After you read

29 Discuss these questions.

    a What happens to these people at the end of the story?

       Milady   d'Artagnan

    b Why does the Cardinal want to be friends with d'Artagnan?

Writing

30 You are d'Artagnan. Write a letter to your parents after your first two or three days in Paris.

31 You work for a Paris newspaper. Write a story about a street fight between the King's musketeers and the Cardinal's guards.

32 The King wants Captain de Tréville to find more musketeers. The Captain writes some ideas on a piece of paper. Write them for him.

    Do you want to fight for your King? Are you ...

33 Life is cheap in this story. Many men die. How do they die? Write about some of them.

34 Constance writes about her feelings at the end of each day. Write about the day of the dance.

35 You are a Huguenot at La Rochelle. You watch the three attacks on the St Gervais bastion. Write about the day.

36 The King and Queen are having tea at the end of the story. They talk about d'Artagnan. Write their conversation.

37 Did you enjoy this story? Why (not)? Write about it.

Answers for the Activities in this book are available from the Pearson English Readers website.
A free Activity Worksheet is also available from the website. Activity worksheets are
part of the Pearson English Readers Teacher Support Programme, which also includes
Progress tests and Graded Reader Guidelines. For more information, please visit:
www.pearsonenglishreaders.com.

WORD LIST *with example sentences*

army (n) He went into the *army* because he wanted to fight for his country.

attack (n/v) After the *attack*, ten people were dead.

bastion (n) They waited in the *bastion* and killed the men on foot below them.

captain (n) The *captain* spoke to his men before the fight began.

The *captain* took the ship south to Argentina.

cardinal (n) He is a *cardinal* in the Catholic Church.

carriage (n) The horses were ready, so the women got into the *carriage*.

diamond (n) She never wears her *diamonds* because she is afraid of losing them.

duke (n) The *Duke* of Edinburgh is Queen Elizabeth II's husband.

guard (n/v) There are *guards* outside the bank all day and all night.

handkerchief (n) Stop crying now! Use my *handkerchief*.

inn (n) People stayed in country *inns* and you could eat there too.

When the *innkeeper* was out, his wife worked behind the bar.

king (n) Please stand up before the *king* comes into the room.

lieutenant (n) He fought well, so they made him a *lieutenant*.

musketeer (n) The *musketeers* will die before they stop fighting.

permit (n) We can't park here. I haven't got a parking *permit*.

piece (n) I'll eat that small *piece* of meat in a sandwich.

pin (n) She wore two beautiful *pins* on her dress.

put money on something He *put* a lot of *money on the black horse* and it won. He is a rich man now.

queen (n) Elizabeth II is the *Queen* of England, Wales, Scotland and Northern Ireland.

sword (n) They fought with *swords*, and the loser died.

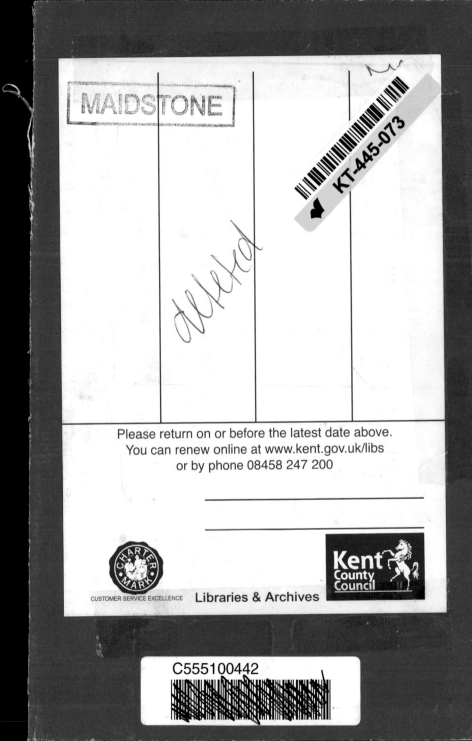

Family Tree

Queen Victoria (1819-1901)
m. Prince Albert of Saxe-Coburg (1819-61)

Edward VII (1841-1910)
m. Princess Alexandra of Denmark (1844-1925)

George V (1865-1936)
m. Princess Victoria Mary of Teck (1867-1953)

Edward VIII	**George VI**	**Prince Henry**	**Prince George**	**Prince John**	**Princess Mary**
(1894-1972)	(1895-1952)	(1900-74)	(1902-42)	(1905-19)	(1897-1965)
m. Mrs Wallis Simpson (1896-1986)	*m. Lady Elizabeth Bowes-Lyon (1900-2002)*	*m. Lady Alice Scott (1901-2004)*	*m. Princess Marina of Greece & Denmark (1906-68)*		*m. The 6th Earl of Harewood (1882-1947)*

Queen Elizabeth II
(b. 1926)
m. Prince Philip, Duke of Edinburgh (b. 1921)

Princess Margaret
(1930-2002)
m. Antony Armstrong-Jones (b.1930) (divorced 1978)

Prince Charles
(b. 1948)
m. (1) Lady Diana Spencer (1961-97)
(2) Mrs Camilla Parker Bowles (b. 1947)

Prince Andrew
(b. 1960)
m. Sarah Ferguson (b. 1959) (divorced 1992)

Prince Edward
(b. 1964)
m. Sophie Rhys-Jones (b. 1965)

Princess Anne
(b. 1950)
m. (1) Captain Mark Phillips (b. 1948)
(2) Vice-Admiral Sir Timothy Laurence (b. 1955)

Prince William
(b. 1982)
m. Catherine Middleton (b. 1982)

Prince Harry
(b. 1984)

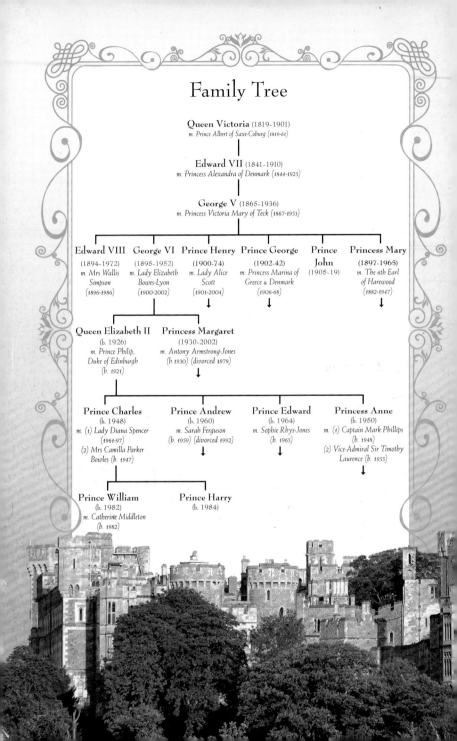

Queen
Elizabeth II

Susanna Davidson

Designed by Karen Tomlins

History consultant: Hugo Vickers

Reading consultant: Alison Kelly
University of Roehampton

Contents

Windsor Castle, one of the Queen's homes, is the oldest and largest occupied castle in the world.

Chapter 1

Happy families

In the early hours of Wednesday April 21, 1926, a royal servant rushed up the stairs and woke the King and Queen to tell them their first granddaughter had been born. "Such relief and joy," Queen Mary wrote in her diary.

No one imagined the newborn princess would one day be queen. Her father, the Duke of York, known as Bertie to his family, was the King's second son. Most people assumed his elder brother, Edward, would become king, and have children of his own.

But this was still a royal baby and Queen Mary was enchanted. "We always wanted a child to make our happiness complete," the Duke of York wrote to his mother a few days later, "and now

The baby Princess Elizabeth with her parents, in her christening gown

that it has at last happened, it seems so
wonderful and strange."

A month later, the baby was christened in a gold
font at Buckingham Palace, dressed in the heavy
satin and lace gown worn by all royal children.
She was named Elizabeth Alexandra Mary, after
her mother, grandmother and great-grandmother.

The baby princess at ten months, with her nanny, 'Allah' Knight. Allah stayed with Princess Elizabeth for nineteen years, until her death in 1945.

Like most rich and aristocratic families at that time, Elizabeth was looked after by a nanny. Clara Knight, known to the family as Allah, believed strongly in order and discipline. The baby princess followed a strict routine and was wheeled out every morning and evening to take the air.

Elizabeth's mother visited the nursery daily and was devoted to her baby, but royal duty came first. In January 1927, when Elizabeth was just nine months old, her parents were sent on a tour of Australia and New Zealand. "I felt very much leaving on Thursday," wrote her mother, "and the baby was so sweet playing with the buttons on Bertie's uniform, it quite broke me up."

When the Duke and Duchess finally returned, Elizabeth was one year and two months old – she had been separated from her parents for almost half her life. They were reunited at Buckingham Palace. When the Duchess saw the baby in her nurse's arms she rushed forward, crying, "Oh you little darling," kissing and hugging her again and again. Then Elizabeth was taken out onto the balcony and held up to cheering crowds.

The Duke and Duchess of York wave from their balcony, shortly after their return from their royal tour. The Duchess is holding Princess Elizabeth.

The family moved to a new house, 145 Piccadilly, where Elizabeth was to spend the next ten years. It lay just across the park from Buckingham Palace, and had five floors, a library, a ballroom, a conservatory and twenty-five bedrooms, most of which were for the servants. Elizabeth, Allah and the nursery-maid, known as Bobo, had a whole floor to themselves – a world safe and secure from all that went on outside.

From the start, the public was fascinated with the young princess. When a magazine wrote that Elizabeth was usually dressed in yellow, children all over the world started to dress in yellow too.

The princess had chocolates, tea sets, hospital wards and even a slice of Antarctica named after her.

The Yorks became the public image of the happy family – an image that was

Princess Elizabeth, at two years old, with her mother

completed by the birth of a second child, Margaret Rose, in August 1930. It was soon clear that the two sisters were total opposites – Elizabeth was sensible and careful, while Margaret was naughty and amusing. The children's governess, Marion Crawford, always known as Crawfie, described how the conscientious Elizabeth would look after her toy horses, grooming, feeding and watering them, before lining up their brushes and pails outside the nursery each night.

The young princesses play in the garden of their grandparents, the Earl and Countess of Strathmore.

Although four years apart, the sisters were always close, with Elizabeth feeling very protective of Margaret. The Duke of York was determined that Margaret should never feel left out, and made sure she was included in everything her sister did. They were even dressed in the same clothes up until their teenage years. 'Us four', the Duke of York called his family, and they were close-knit and contented.

This photograph shows the royal family at their country home, the Royal Lodge, in Windsor.

Princess Elizabeth stands with her grandparents on Buckingham Palace balcony. You can just see Princess Margaret's head as she peers over the edge.

Elizabeth was close to her grandparents too, particularly the King, George V, who gave her the nickname 'Lilibet'. He also gave Elizabeth her first pony, a Shetland called Peggy, for her fourth birthday.

That same day she walked across the square at Windsor Castle, in a yellow coat trimmed with fur. A band played and she waved at the surging crowds, while the women blew back kisses. In these early years of her life, Elizabeth was learning what it meant to be royal.

Princess Elizabeth sits next to her grandmother, Queen Mary, on their way to a ceremony at St. James's Palace, London. Her mother sits opposite and her aunt, Princess Mary, is beside her.

Elizabeth could see the deference with which people treated the King and Queen, and from the age of three was curtseying to them herself.

From her grandmother, Queen Mary, she learned that there were strict codes of royal conduct. On a trip to a concert, Elizabeth fidgeted so much the Queen asked her if she wanted to go home. "Oh no, Granny," Elizabeth said, "we can't leave before the end. Think of all the people who'll be waiting to see us outside." Queen Mary thought she was being big-headed, and sent her home in disgrace.

In 1935, Elizabeth experienced the grandeur of a royal occasion with her grandfather's Silver Jubilee, a huge event celebrating his twenty-five years on the throne. Elizabeth and her sister, dressed in matching pink, drove through the cheering crowds in an open carriage to St. Paul's Cathedral.

A souvenir card celebrating King George V's Silver Jubilee

The royal carriage can be seen here, leaving Buckingham Palace on the day of the Silver Jubilee.

A crowd looks on as the princesses
arrive at an event in London, in 1936.

The princesses were discovering how different
they were to ordinary people, and it made them
all the more fascinated by them, especially other
children. Their governess, Crawfie, noticed how,
"The little girls used to smile shyly at those they
liked the look of. They would so have loved to
speak to them and make friends, but this was
never encouraged."

Princesses Elizabeth and Margaret enjoy a trip to London Zoo with their governess, Crawfie, in 1938. Elizabeth is third from the left, Margaret is second from the right.

Crawfie began to try to take them on trips into the 'ordinary world' but this soon proved too difficult. On one occasion they went by underground to a canteen. Elizabeth left her pot of tea behind on the counter and was shouted at by the woman serving. But they were soon recognized, and attracted so much attention their detective had to call up a car to take them back, so they could escape from the gathering crowds.

Unlike many royal children, however, Elizabeth and Margaret spent a lot of time with both their parents. The Duke and Duchess visited their children each morning, before they took lessons with their governesses, and at the end of the day they would play cards and have pillow fights until it was time for bed. "In those days we lived in an ivory tower," Crawfie wrote later, "removed from the real world." But the ivory tower could not last. There was a royal storm brewing outside which was set to change their lives forever.

Princess Elizabeth stands in front of her miniature house in the gardens of the Royal Lodge. It was given to her by the people of Wales.

Chapter 2

Heir to the throne

The year Elizabeth turned ten, the family spent Christmas together. King George V was clearly very ill and died a month later. Elizabeth went to his funeral at Windsor Castle, dressed in a new black coat and velvet beret, clutching her mother's hand as the coffin was lowered into the Royal Vault.

George V's funeral procession in London, 1936

At first, little changed in the lives of the princesses. There was now a new king on the throne, their father's brother, King Edward VIII. The public adored him. He had been their golden-haired prince and now he was their young and popular King. But there was a secret hanging over him, kept out of the press and mentioned only in whispers, which was threatening to bring his reign to an abrupt end. Edward was in love with a twice-divorced American woman, Wallis Simpson.

Edward VIII and Wallis, sightseeing together in Croatia, in 1936

Edward VIII broadcasts to the British Empire that he will abdicate.

Divorce was heavily frowned upon then
– particularly in royal circles – and it was
unthinkable that Edward could marry Wallis and
make her his queen.

On October 27, 1936, the newspapers broke
the scandal. Given the choice between marrying
the woman he loved or remaining King, Edward
VIII chose love. When the Duke of York told
his mother what had happened he broke down
and sobbed like a child. Before the end of the
year Edward had abdicated, and Elizabeth's
father became King George VI.

The shock was almost too much for the new King. He was a shy man, his shyness made worse by a stammer that made public speaking a nightmare for him, and he had never wanted to be king. Edward's abdication destroyed the brothers' friendship and he was rarely spoken of by Elizabeth's parents again.

For Elizabeth, the realization that she might one day become Queen came gradually. According to her other grandmother, Lady Strathmore, Princess Elizabeth prayed nightly for a brother to take her place as next in line to the throne.

The royal family gather on the balcony of Buckingham Palace after the Coronation ceremony.

"When our father became King," Princess Margaret recalled, "I said to her, 'Does that mean you're going to be Queen?' She replied, 'Yes, I suppose it does.' She didn't mention it again."

Buckingham Palace in 1937 – the flag is flying to show the royal family is in residence.

Any sense of private life was now over. The family moved to Buckingham Palace, where crowds gathered daily outside the railings, hoping to catch a glimpse of them. But for the princesses, it was fun too. "People need bicycles in this place," Elizabeth declared, and Margaret would often ride her tricycle up and down the long palace corridors.

The princesses could no longer take walks in the park or play with the children next-door, but they loved the gardens at Buckingham Palace.

Elizabeth's mother soon made the palace rooms as homely as possible. Elizabeth had a sitting-room of her own, while their schoolroom looked out over the palace gardens. The King set up the children's rocking-horses outside his study so he could hear them play as he worked.

Elizabeth no longer referred to her parents as Mummy and Papa, but spoke of them as the King and Queen. The Queen also insisted on adding a 'touch of majesty' to the nursery, which involved their meals being served by two footmen in scarlet uniform.

This photograph shows the princesses accompanying their parents on an inspection at the Palace of Holyroodhouse, in Edinburgh.

Outside Buckingham Palace, Princesses Elizabeth and Margaret watch a regiment being presented with a new flag, known as a standard.

The princesses' lives were now surrounded by pomp and ceremony, which soon seemed normal to them. They were attended by a swarm of staff, and there were also endless formal occasions. At the State Opening of Parliament, the princesses watched as their parents put on their crowns and sat on thrones.

Now that Elizabeth was heir to the throne, her parents began to take her education more seriously. She was taught Latin, European history and the history of the monarchy.

Here you can see Princess Elizabeth as a Girl Guide and Princess Margaret as a Brownie.

Elizabeth also began to join her parents when diplomats and foreign heads of state were visiting.

So that they could still mix with 'ordinary' children, there was a meeting of Girl Guides and Brownies at Buckingham Palace every Wednesday, although all the children involved were also from privileged backgrounds. Elizabeth was described by her cousin, Patricia Mountbatten, as "nice, easy to deal with, you'd want her as your best friend." Already, there was something different about her though. "For instance, she couldn't burst into tears. If she hurt her knee she knew she must try not to cry."

In many ways, Elizabeth was a country girl at heart. She adored her family's weekend trips to Windsor and the summer holidays spent at Balmoral Castle in Scotland. At twelve, she told her riding teacher that if she hadn't been a princess, "I'd like to be a lady living in the country with lots of horses and dogs."

Princess Elizabeth and her father both shared a passion for horses.

Elizabeth remained fascinated by life outside the royal bubble. Years later, when having her portrait painted in the Yellow Drawing Room in Buckingham Palace, she recalled how she had spent hours in the room as a child, looking out of the windows. "I loved watching the people and the cars… They all seemed so busy. I used to wonder what they were doing and where they were all going, and what they thought about outside the Palace."

In 1939, the royal family spent the summer as usual at Balmoral, but their holiday was brought to an abrupt end when the King was summoned to London. He was swiftly followed by the Queen. A few days later, it was announced that Great Britain was at war with Germany.

The first tragedy to strike Elizabeth was the sinking of a battleship, *Royal Oak*, in which 800 sailors died. At Christmas, the princesses were reunited with their parents, but Elizabeth felt guilty about enjoying herself. "Perhaps we were too happy," she wrote to Crawfie. "I kept thinking of those sailors and what Christmas must have been like in their homes."

As German troops swept across Europe, the country was faced with the terrifying threat of invasion. The children and Crawfie were evacuated to Windsor Castle, where they were to stay for five years. The King and Queen remained in London during the day, even as the bombs began to fall, determined to share the dangers faced by their people.

The King and Queen visit a bombed area of the East End of London, in April 1941.

Princess Elizabeth makes her first radio broadcast, alongside her sister Margaret, in 1940. The speech was addressed to all the children of the Commonwealth, many of whom had been sent away during the war.

As part of the war effort, the princesses collected tinfoil, rolled bandages and knitted socks for the forces, and Elizabeth made her first radio broadcast. Despite the mayhem and chaos that surrounded them, the princesses were protected at the Castle, and Elizabeth loved being surrounded by a sense of history. One of Elizabeth's friends described it as having, "a happy family atmosphere."

But Elizabeth was longing for more freedom and the chance to 'do her bit' for the war effort as her friends were. Her father would not allow it. He felt very protective, and as Elizabeth grew older, she found his protectiveness frustrating. "I ought to do as other girls do," she said.

Instead, she spent her time being groomed for her future as Queen, which included meeting any important visitors who came to stay. When Eleanor Roosevelt, wife of the US President, visited in 1942, she described the sixteen-year-old Elizabeth as, "quite serious with a great deal of character and personality. She asked me a number of questions about life in the United States and they were serious questions."

The same year, Elizabeth also inspected a regiment for the first time, which she found "a bit frightening... but it was not as bad as I expected it to be."

In the spring of 1945, just before her nineteenth birthday, she was at last allowed 'out' to join the Auxiliary Territorial Service. For perhaps the only time in her life, she was able to work alongside ordinary people, learning to drive and mend a car.

Dressed in her ATS uniform, Princess Elizabeth tinkers with an engine of a car as she does her mechanical training during the war.

At first, Elizabeth felt shy, but she soon started to talk to the other girls, who were all very interested to meet her. "Quite striking," one girl wrote in her diary at the time, "short pretty brown crisp curly hair. Lovely grey-blue eyes, and an extremely charming smile, and she uses lipstick!"

Elizabeth's experience of mixing with other girls was short-lived. The course came to an end, and soon after, so did the war. As everyone celebrated, Elizabeth and Margaret slipped out of the palace and mingled with the crowds, unrecognized. Years later, Elizabeth remembered, "lines of people linking arms and walking down Whitehall, and all of us were swept along by tides of happiness and relief." The end of the war was also to mark the end of Elizabeth's seclusion, and her girlhood.

Thousands of Londoners gather outside Buckingham Palace to celebrate the end of the war in Europe.

Chapter 3

Love & marriage

Princess Elizabeth and Prince Philip
on honeymoon, in November 1947.

Princess Elizabeth first met Prince Philip
of Greece when she was just thirteen, and
he eighteen, at the Royal Naval College at
Dartmouth, where Philip was training as a cadet.
Philip was tall and handsome, with blond hair
and striking features. For Elizabeth, it was a case
of love at first sight.

Philip spent much of the war fighting at sea,
but he saw Elizabeth whenever he was on leave
in London. In 1944, Queen Mary had confided
to an old friend that Elizabeth and Philip had,

"been in love for the past eighteen months. In fact longer, I think… But the King and Queen… want her to see more of the world before committing herself." Queen Mary also admitted that it seemed as if Elizabeth had made up her mind. "There's something very steadfast and determined in her – like her father."

When Prince Philip proposed at Balmoral in 1946, Elizabeth instantly accepted. The King, however, couldn't bear the thought that 'us four' were already to be parted. He made Elizabeth promise that nothing would be official until her twenty-first birthday, and that first the family would go on a tour together, to South Africa.

Princess Elizabeth plays deck games with the crew during the royal family's trip to South Africa.

South Africa was Elizabeth's first experience of the British Commonwealth, the countries that made up, or had once been part of, the British Empire. She had her twenty-first birthday on tour, and marked it with a speech, dedicated to all the people of the Commonwealth. "It is very simple," she said. "I declare before you all that my whole life... shall be devoted to your service and the service of our great Imperial family to which we all belong..." Elizabeth read the words with real earnestness and sincerity, bringing, it was said, "a lump into millions of throats."

On their return, the engagement was announced and they married on a dark November day. Elizabeth wore a fairy-princess dress in ivory silk covered with white roses sewn from pearls. Wedding presents and royalty came from all over the world and for a week there were rounds of parties – a splash of gaiety in the drab post-war world.

Princess Elizabeth and Prince Philip, in his naval uniform, at Buckingham Palace on their wedding day

George VI was deeply moved by the wedding service. While Elizabeth was on honeymoon, he wrote to tell her how he felt.

> I was so proud of you... but when I handed your hand to the Archbishop I felt that I had lost something very precious... do remember that your old home is still yours & do come back to it as much & as often as possible. I can see that you are sublimely happy with Philip which is right but don't forget us is the wish of Your ever loving & devoted Papa.

Crowds line the streets to watch the wedding procession.

Elizabeth and Philip smile for the cameras on their way back from an official engagement.

Elizabeth and Philip, now known as the Duke and Duchess of Edinburgh, returned home from honeymoon to take up their public duties. They visited Paris on an official tour, where they were a great success, described by one onlooker as a divine couple.

In November 1948, Elizabeth gave birth to their first child, HRH Prince Charles Philip Arthur George. When the announcement was made, a huge crowd gathered outside the palace, and the cheering lasted until after midnight.

A few months later, Elizabeth and Philip were able to move into their new home, Clarence House, where they were extremely happy. Philip helped to give his new wife confidence. "She was marvellous at doing her duties," one of her ladies-in-waiting recalled, but "she really was agonizingly shy."

Philip, however, was longing to go back to sea and that year they went out to Malta, where Philip was posted aboard HMS *Chequers*. The baby was left behind with his nannies and grandparents, just as Elizabeth had been left as a baby by her own parents.

Princess Elizabeth gazes at her month-old son.

Princess Elizabeth visits her husband, the Duke of Edinburgh, in Malta in 1949, where the Duke was stationed with the Royal Navy.

In Malta, Elizabeth was able to lead an almost ordinary life, as a naval officer's wife. There was no press to put on a show for, and instead she could go shopping or out to the hairdressers. "They were so relaxed and free, coming and going as they pleased..." recalled a member of their staff. "I think it was their happiest time."

But, after two years, the King's health began to fail. Elizabeth and Philip had to return to England to take on some of his duties. By now, they had two children, Charles and Anne. This wasn't allowed to interfere with Elizabeth's royal duties, however. In 1951, it was decided that the Edinburghs should go on a tour of Australia and New Zealand, in the place of the King and Queen. They were to stop off first in Kenya, to stay at a lodge they had been given as a wedding present.

The King went with them to the airport. Before they left, he said to Bobo, a trusted servant, "Look after the Princess for me." Six days later, he was dead, of a heart attack in his sleep. He was only fifty-six. Elizabeth had left the country a princess. She would return to it as Queen.

King George VI, with hand raised, waves goodbye to his daughter.

Chapter 4

Head of State

Elizabeth, now Queen Elizabeth II,
arriving back from Kenya

On the flight back from Kenya, Elizabeth appeared calm to those around her, although one member of staff saw her get up once or twice and return to her seat, looking as if she'd been crying. The change in her and Philip's position was immediate. Gone was their independence or any sense of freedom. It was time to take up the reins of duty.

Her grandmother, Queen Mary, came to see her shortly after she arrived home, and met her with a curtsey. "Her old Grannie and subject must be the first to kiss Her hand," she said, much to Elizabeth's dismay.

Still in shock over her father's death, Elizabeth had no time to grieve. The following morning she had to go to the meeting of her Accession Council, where she had formally to declare herself Queen.

"My heart is too full for me to say more to you today than that I shall always work as my father did," she said simply. On the way back in the car with Philip, she finally broke down and sobbed.

But Elizabeth was also helped out of her sadness by her new role. "Mummy and Margaret have the biggest grief to bear, for their future must seem very blank, while I have a job and a family to think of," Elizabeth wrote. She was enjoying her new responsibilities and looking ahead to her Coronation in Westminster Abbey when she would be publicly crowned Queen. There would be celebrations across the nation, from village carnivals to street parties.

As the Coronation date drew near, Elizabeth rehearsed her lines, with sheets pinned to her shoulders so she could get used to the cumbersome robes she would have to wear.

On the day itself, crowds lined the streets, cheering despite the drizzling rain. Elizabeth, in a white satin dress with a red velvet train, waved to them all on her way to the Abbey, a radiant smile on her face. In front of millions of television viewers, the Archbishop presented the public with their new Queen. The congregation roared, "God Save Queen Elizabeth".

The whole ceremony had an ancient air, filled with slow and stately movement, sparkling jewels and solemn vows. For Elizabeth, it was a spiritual rite of passage, as she dedicated her life to that of her people.

Just five months after the coronation, Elizabeth and Philip set out on a six-month tour of the Commonwealth. Elizabeth was to travel more than any other monarch in history. She and Philip frequently sailed aboard the royal yacht, *Britannia*, furnished inside to look like a country house at sea. Here, the royal family could entertain heads of state as well as relaxing after a long day.

Elizabeth took her role as Head of the Commonwealth seriously, but the tours were often long and tiring, and fraught with risk. In 1961, five days before she was due to sail to Ghana, in Africa, two bombs exploded in the capital, Accra. But Elizabeth insisted on going, determined to help keep the country within the Commonwealth, as it was becoming increasingly close to Communist Russia. "She loves her duty and means to be a Queen and not a puppet," the Prime Minister wrote in his diary.

Even at home, the Queen's work never ceased.

The Queen and Prince Philip on their tour of Ghana, driving through the dusty streets to greet the people.

From the beginning, state papers were delivered to her daily in leather-covered boxes. She studied them carefully, and was quick to catch out her Prime Ministers at their weekly meetings if they hadn't read their briefs. One Prime Minster, Harold Macmillan, wrote, "I was astonished at Her Majesty's grasp of all the details."

There was one side of the job that Elizabeth did find a struggle – public speaking. Her honesty meant she found it difficult to say anything she didn't believe and she always read her speeches, which made them sound less spontaneous. A naturally shy person, public occasions were something the Queen did as her duty, rather than a thing to be enjoyed.

As she grew into her role of Queen, a gap was opening up, between her public image, serious and dignified, and Elizabeth's private self. "When she smiles, the whole face comes to life," a relation said. "She loves a good laugh – I've seen the Queen laugh till the tears ran down her face..." One of her fashion advisers described how, "The woman I see is full of jokes... and only too ready to laugh at anything – particularly herself. If only people could see her as she is."

As time passed, Elizabeth found there were great shifts in the public's attitude to the monarchy. She became subject to criticism in the press, from articles abroad claiming she didn't smile enough on state visits, to uproar at home over the amount of money spent on the royal family. Nor was there a time when she could take a day off from being Queen. As a way to relax, she pursued her other interests when she could – country walks, breeding gundogs and her real passion, breeding racehorses. She has been amazingly successful at it, her horses having won nearly all the important races.

The Queen with her first classic racehorse winner at Epsom, in 1957

The Queen was surprised and touched by the crowds that gathered for her Silver Jubilee, in 1977. It was a difficult time for the country, with rising unemployment and little money to spare for celebrations. But, in spite of everything, it was one of the high points of her reign.

There were bonfires and street parties, and hundreds of ordinary people lined the streets to see her as she toured the country. "She could not believe that people had that much affection for her as a person," said her domestic chaplain, "and she was embarrassed and at the same time terribly touched by it all."

The Queen wanted to mark her Jubilee by meeting as many people as possible. Here she greets people on the streets of Camberwell, London.

Elizabeth visited Northern Ireland in her Jubilee year, even though the violence there between Catholics and Protestants put her life in danger. "We said we're going to Ulster," she told her Private Secretary, "and it would be a great pity not to."

The Queen had come to represent something – a symbol of continuity, a focus for the nation, an upholder of the values of courage and decency. And this is what had brought people out of their homes and onto the streets, just to catch a glimpse of her.

At a street party in Belfast, Northern Ireland, during the Queen's Silver Jubilee, children wave the Union Jack flag as a sign of loyalty to the Queen.

Chapter 5

Family strife

Elizabeth couldn't help but be an absent mother. Her tours of the Commonwealth meant she had been away for much of Charles and Anne's childhood, often over birthdays and once over Christmas, too. When at home, though, she kept an hour for the children in the morning and another at bath time. When Charles caught chickenpox, she was unable to see him because of the risk of infection. But, as soon as he had recovered, she refused invitations so she could be with him. Philip, too, made sure he was there to read and play with the children at bedtime.

In 1960, Elizabeth gave birth to another child, Prince Andrew, followed by Prince Edward four years later. "Goodness what fun it is to have a baby in the house again!" she told a friend after Edward was born. "He is a great joy to us all..."

Elizabeth always struggled to protect her children from the press, but her advisers were worried that the monarchy was starting to seem old-fashioned and out of touch. In 1969, for the first time, television cameras were allowed behind the scenes to follow the royal family for a year.

The film showed a happy, wholesome and united family, portraying the royals as ordinary human beings. But there was danger too, as the film made the public more intrigued than ever about the family's personal lives.

By the 1970s, the family was growing apart. Charles had joined the navy, Anne was married, and the younger two were away at school. They were talking less and only really meeting for formal occasions.

A family portrait taken on holiday at Balmoral, Scotland

Prince Charles kisses his bride on the balcony of Buckingham Palace, in front of cheering crowds.

Then, in 1981, Charles was married, to Lady Diana Spencer. The wedding was portrayed as a fairy-tale match on the television, as was Prince Andrew's wedding to Sarah Ferguson in 1986.

The way the newspapers reported the monarchy was also beginning to change. Instead of surrounding them with respect and a sense of mystery, people were being given endless details about every aspect of their lives. The royals had been admired for representing an ideal family, but as their personal lives unravelled in the late 1980s, the press began to turn.

They reported on the rocky relationships within the marriages of the younger royals. If the royal family didn't uphold standards, what was it for?

Things did not get better. The Queen described 1992 as her 'annus horribilis', the Latin for 'horrible year'. The announcement that Prince Andrew was to separate from his wife was swiftly followed by Princess Anne's divorce. In June, a book was published detailing the unhappy marriage of Charles and Diana. In November that year, a fire broke out at Windsor Castle, the Queen's childhood home. No one was killed, but the fire caused terrible damage. The Queen was devastated.

Smoke and flames flood the night sky above Windsor Castle. It took nine hours to bring the fire under control.

At first, people reacted sympathetically, but there was an uproar when it was suggested the public should pay for the repair. Then, in December, it was announced that Charles and Diana were to separate.

The Queen responded to the criticism. The monarchy decided to begin paying tax, like the rest of the public, and Buckingham Palace was opened to the public, to help pay for the repairs to Windsor Castle. But while there was still a great deal of respect for the Queen, and a recognition of how well she did her job, the criticism did not go away. Some newspapers painted her as a cold and unfeeling mother and as being out of touch with the public. Through it all, the Queen carried on, doing her job as she had always done – reading and signing papers, giving speeches, meeting people, visiting and touring. "The Queen's strength," said one of her aides, "is that she doesn't change very much."

Then tragedy struck. On August 31, 1997,
Princess Diana was killed in a car crash in Paris.
The nation went into shock, followed by a public
outpouring of grief never seen before. People
came in their thousands to lay flowers outside
Kensington Palace, where she had lived, and
waited for hours to sign books with messages
of love and remembrance.

The Queen was staying at Balmoral in Scotland
at the time, and remained there, looking after
Charles and Diana's children, Prince William and

The Queen and Prince Philip
look at the tributes left for Diana
outside Buckingham Palace.

Prince Harry. But the public's grief quickly turned to anger, the Queen's absence from London seen as evidence of her uncaring attitude to Diana. The newspapers demanded the Union flag be flown at Buckingham Palace at half-mast, as a sign of respect to Diana, and that the Queen come and talk to her people.

Diana's brother, Earl Spencer, Prince William and Harry and their father, Prince Charles, at Diana's funeral

In the face of such anger, the Queen was forced to comply. She left Balmoral for London, and as she arrived at the palace, the crowds began to clap. That evening, Elizabeth went on television to speak about Diana. "I for one," she said, "believe that there are lessons to be drawn from her life and from the extraordinary and moving reaction to her death." To survive, the monarchy was going to have to change.

Chapter 6

A job for life

The Queen's approach to change had always been cautious, unwilling to abandon the traditions and customs followed by her own parents. Following Diana's death, however, she seemed more open to suggestion and ready to take on some of the ways Diana had performed her role – being more informal, and having more direct contact with ordinary people, in ordinary places.

Here the Queen makes an informal visit to a primary school in Northern Ireland.

Her days were arranged differently, so she spent more time talking to the people she met on her visits. She was shown keeping up with the times, smiling more for the cameras and speaking more about current concerns.

The new-style 'modern' monarchy was put to the test in 1999, when Australia held a vote to decide if, as a member of the Commonwealth, it wanted to keep the Queen as Head of State. Everyone expected Australia to vote to become a republic, but instead just over half the Australian people voted to keep the Queen.

The Queen accepts flowers from schoolgirls in Canberra, Australia, in 2000. The Queen has made sixteen visits to Australia during her reign.

The royal family's popularity was given a further boost, as attention shifted away from the Queen's children to her grandchildren. In 2000, Prince William, like many other teenagers leaving school, went on a gap year, doing charitable work both in the UK and abroad. Images of the prince cleaning toilets on a project in South America put across the idea of the royal family as increasingly in touch with the lives of ordinary people.

Prince William, on his gap year in Chile, makes a wooden rubbish bin for the local villagers.

The year of the Queen's Golden Jubilee, 2002, celebrated her fifty years on the throne. But it began with two great losses for the Queen – the death of her sister, Princess Margaret, in February, followed by that of her mother less than two months later, at the age of 101.

The Queen Mother with her two daughters on her 100th birthday

Two hundred thousand people came to pay their respects to the Queen Mother, walking past her coffin as it lay in state in Westminster Hall. Despite this profound show of loyalty and affection, many newspapers predicted that the Golden Jubilee would be a failure, claiming that the British public was no longer interested in the monarchy.

They were proved wrong, as hundreds of thousands thronged to fêtes up and down the country, while a million people came to the parade in the Mall, in London.

With the wedding of Prince William and Catherine Middleton in April 2011, the royal family seemed once again to be riding a wave of popularity. Over 24 million people tuned in to watch the wedding on television in the UK, with millions more watching around the world.

Away from the pomp and finery of grand royal occasions, the Queen, now in her eighties, continues to work hard at her job. At a time of life when most people are settled in their retirement, she shows the same energy and determination in fulfilling her duties as she has always done. In May 2011, she made a historic visit to the Republic of Ireland, the first British monarch to visit the country since 1911.

Prince William and his bride, now the Duchess of Cambridge, smile and wave at the crowds from the balcony at Buckingham Palace.

Despite the risk from republican terrorists, the Queen spent her four-day visit commemorating the lives that had been lost in the struggles between the two countries, cementing a new era of friendship between them.

The Queen has described her role as "a job for life". A lonely one at times, but helped, she has said, by her husband, whom she has called "my strength and stay all these years".

Through all the ups and downs the monarchy has faced, the Queen has never stopped working. Her oath to serve her country, which she took at the age of twenty-five, was a heartfelt one, holding true over fifty years later.

2012 is the year of the Queen's Diamond Jubilee, celebrating her sixty years on the throne. It makes her the second-longest serving monarch in British history. Her reign has seen twelve British Prime Ministers come and go and she remains a popular Head of State to fifteen Commonwealth countries. Whatever the future holds for the monarchy, the Queen's reign will be remembered for her dignity and her devotion to the role. As Sir Winston Churchill, her very first Prime Minister, said of her, "I became conscious of the Royal resolve to serve as well as rule, and indeed to rule by serving."

The Queen in April 2011,
attending a service at
Windsor Castle

ACKNOWLEDGEMENTS

© akg-images p9; © Camera Press front cover (Lord Snowdon), p44 (John Bulmer); © Corbis spine (Hulton-Deutsch Collection), p15 (Hulton-Deutsch Collection), p56 (PAUL MCERLANE/epa); © Getty Images pp2-3 (Scott E Barbour/Image Bank), p5, p6, p7, p8 (Popperfoto), p10, p12, p13(tr) (Popperfoto), p13(b), p14, p16, p17, p20, p21, p22, p23, p24 (Time & Life Pictures), p25 (Gamma-Keystone), p28, p30 (Popperfoto), p31 (SSPL), p32, p33 (Popperfoto), p34 (via Gamma-Keystone), p35, p37 (Gamma-Keystone), p39 (Popperfoto), p40 (AFP), p46, p47, p50 (Lichfield), p55, p58 (Tim Graham), p63; © Press Association Images p11 (AP/AP), p18 (Topham/ Topham Picturepoint), p19 (PA/PA Archive), p27 (/S&G Barratts/EMPICS Archive), p43 (PA/PA Archive), p51 (PA/PA Archive), pp60-1 (Chris Ison/ PA Wire); © Rex Features p52, p54, p59 (Mike Forster/Daily Mail); © Topfoto.co.uk p36 (AP), p38 (2005), p48 (2002, Topham Picturepoint), p57 (Topham/PA); © V&A Images p1

Please note some of the black and white images in the
book have been digitally tinted by Usborne.

Internet links

You can find out more about the Queen by
going to the Usborne Quicklinks website at
www.usborne-quicklinks.com
and typing the keywords "the queen".

Edited by Jane Chisholm

Digital manipulation by Keith Furnival

With thanks to Ruth King for her help with picture research

First published in 2012 by Usborne Publishing Ltd., Usborne House,
83-85 Saffron Hill, London EC1N 8RT, England. www.usborne.com
Copyright © 2012 Usborne Publishing Ltd.